The Mysterious Footprint

"The Frisbee landed under one of those bushes," Jason said. "When I went to get it, I found something totally amazing."

Mike kneeled in front of a bush. He brushed aside some branches and pointed to a flat rock on the ground. "Is that awesome or what?" he asked.

Nancy looked down. In the rock was an outline of a footprint. A giant footprint!

Nancy couldn't stop staring. The footprint was about two feet long and eight inches wide. It had three pointy toes.

"What do you think it is?" she asked. "Some kind of bear?"

"Du-uh!" Jason said. "It's a dinosaur!"

The Nancy Drew Notebooks

Available from MINSTREL Books

THE
NANCY DREW
NOTEBOOKS®

#40

Dinosaur Alert!

CAROLYN KEENE
ILLUSTRATED BY JAN NAIMO JONES

A MINSTREL®
BOOK

Published by POCKET BOOKS
New York   London   Toronto   Sydney   Singapore

This book is a work of fiction. Names, characters, places and incidents are products of the author's imagination or are used fictitiously. Any resemblance to actual events or locales or persons living or dead is entirely coincidental.

A MINSTREL PAPERBACK *Original*

A Minstrel Book published by
POCKET BOOKS, a division of Simon & Schuster, Inc.
1230 Avenue of the Americas, New York, NY 10020

ISBN: 0-7434-0663-X

First Minstrel Books printing February 2001

10 9 8 7 6 5 4 3 2 1

NANCY DREW, THE NANCY DREW NOTEBOOKS, A MINSTREL BOOK and colophon are registered trademarks of Simon & Schuster, Inc.

Cover art by Joanie Schwarz

Printed in the U.S.A.

PHX/

Dinosaur Alert!

1
Mystery Message

I wonder who invented pizza," eight-year-old Nancy Drew said on the lunch line. It was Tuesday—and Tuesday was pizza day at Carl Sandburg Elementary School.

"Probably the same person who invented the bicycle," Nancy's best friend George Fayne said.

Bess Marvin looked puzzled. She was George's cousin and Nancy's other best friend. "The bicycle?" she asked. "Why?"

"So he could deliver!" George joked.

Nancy giggled and pushed her tray along the metal ledge. Just then a boy from the first grade rushed over.

"Are you Nancy Drew?" he asked.

"That's me," Nancy replied.

"Cool." The boy tossed a note on Nancy's tray. "Jason Hutchings told me to give you this note. He said read it. Then destroy it."

Nancy rolled her eyes. Jason and his friends Mike Minelli and David Berger were the biggest pests in their third-grade class. They were always making trouble for Nancy, Bess, and George.

The boy smiled mischievously. "Is it a love note?" he snickered.

"Ewwww!" Bess cried.

"Go away!" George told the boy.

The boy ran to the back of the lunch line. Nancy reached for the note, but George grabbed her hand.

"Don't touch it, Nancy!" George cried. Her dark eyes flashed. "The boys might have stuck a wad of gum inside. Or worse!"

"I can't just ignore it," Nancy said. "Even if it is from the boys."

"Why not?" Bess asked.

"Because I'm a detective," Nancy said.

"And a good detective always investigates everything."

Bess and George both nodded.

Nancy was the best detective at school. She even had a blue detective notebook where she wrote all her clues.

Nancy unfolded the note and began to read out it loud: "'Meet us in back of the school during recess. Come alone.' Signed, 'Jason, David, and Mike.'"

What's in back of the school? Nancy wondered. And why do I have to come alone?

"You're not going, are you, Nancy?" Bess asked. Her blue eyes were flashing.

"The boys will probably throw Squirmy Wormies in your hair," George said.

Nancy shuddered. Squirmy Wormies were sticky toy worms that the boys liked to throw against the walls—and on girls.

Nancy stuck out her chin. "I'm not afraid of Jason, David, and Mike," she said. "Besides—"

"—A good detective investigates everything," Bess and George said at the same time.

"Next!" Mrs. Carmichael, the lunch lady, called out.

"That's us!" George said excitedly.

The girls quickly slid their trays up to Mrs. Carmichael.

"Three slices of pizza, coming up," Mrs. Carmichael said. She was wearing her usual hairnet and a uniform with her name, *Enid*, stitched over the front pocket.

"And three fruit salads, too," Bess said. She twirled her blond ponytail.

George nudged her cousin.

"Please," Bess added.

"Sorry, girls," Mrs. Carmichael said. "No fruit salad today."

"But I said please," Bess said.

Mrs. Carmichael smiled. "I'm saving all the fruit for Friday. That's the day of the Carl Sandburg Reunion Breakfast."

"What's a reunion?" George asked.

"It's a party for people who used to go to this school," Mrs. Carmichael explained. "People like me and Alice Stone, the reporter. You remember her, don't you?"

Nancy nodded. Then she tried to imagine Mrs. Carmichael as a third grader. What was her favorite subject? Did she eat pizza on Tuesdays, too?

"I'm in charge of the refreshments," Mrs. Carmichael added. "I'm cooking French toast and scrambled eggs. And I'm spelling out Carl Sandburg with fish sticks."

"We want pizza! We want pizza!" some kids called from the lunch line.

Mrs. Carmichael handed Nancy, Bess, and George three slices and three banana puddings. Then the girls carried their trays to the rows of tables.

Nancy saw Jason, David, and Mike at their usual table by the window. They were staring at Nancy and whispering.

They're definitely up to something, Nancy thought. But what?

All through lunch Nancy couldn't think of anything but the mysterious note.

When it was time for recess Bess and George wished Nancy luck. She walked around the school to the back. Alone.

"Jason?" Nancy called. She stood in the grassy yard surrounded by bushes and a chain fence. "David? Mike?"

No answer.

Oh, well, Nancy thought. Maybe Bess and George were right. Maybe it was just—

"Yo!"

Nancy's reddish blond hair bounced as she spun around. The boys were standing right behind her.

"Did we scare you?" Jason asked.

"You *surprised* me," Nancy corrected him. "Now, what is this all about?"

"First you have to promise not to tell anyone," Mike said.

Nancy rolled her eyes. "I can't promise until I know what I'm promising."

The boys nodded at one another. Then Jason began to speak: "Yesterday after school we were playing with my new electronic supersonic Frisbee. I threw it really hard and David missed it."

"Did not!" David said. "It was Mike."

"Nuh-uh!" Mike said.

"Whatever!" Jason snapped. "The Frisbee landed under one of those bushes."

Nancy glanced at the bushes in front of the fence.

"When I went to get it," Jason went on, "I found something totally amazing."

"Check it out," Mike said.

Nancy followed the boys. Mike kneeled in front of a bush. He brushed aside some branches and pointed to a flat rock on the ground. "Is that awesome or what?" he asked.

Nancy looked down. In the rock was an outline of a footprint. A giant footprint!

Nancy couldn't stop staring. The footprint was about two feet long and eight inches wide. It had three pointy toes.

"What do you think it is?" she asked. "Some kind of . . . bear?"

The boys laughed.

"Du-uh," Jason said. "It's a dinosaur!"

"A what?" Nancy cried. She had learned about dinosaurs in school. They had lived on earth millions of years ago. They were extinct.

"A dinosaur," Mike said. He began to spell. "D-i-n-o-s-o-r-e."

"That's not how you spell *dinosaur*," Nancy said. "And there *were* no dinosaurs in River Heights."

"How do you know?" David demanded.

"They've never found any dinosaur fossils in town," Nancy said.

"Until *now*," Mike said.

"This is a real dinosaur fossil," Jason said proudly. "And we found it."

"And when people find out that we found it—we'll be famous," David said.

Nancy didn't really believe the footprint was a dinosaur's. There had to be some kind of explanation.

"Why don't you show it to someone at the River Heights Museum?" she suggested.

"No way!" Jason exclaimed. "We want to make sure it's a dinosaur footprint before we show it to anyone."

"How are you going to do that?" Nancy asked.

"*We* won't," Jason said with a grin. "But *you* will!"

2

An Awesome Offer

Me?" Nancy cried. "You want me to prove that it's a dinosaur footprint?"

"You *are* the school's best detective," Mike said in a sneering voice. "Detectives always study footprints."

"Not giant footprints with three toes!" Nancy exclaimed. She turned to walk away. "Sorry. I can't help you."

Jason cleared his throat. "You will . . . when you hear our offer."

"Offer?" Nancy stopped walking. "What offer?"

Jason gave a sly smile. "If you investigate this footprint and prove it's a dinosaur's, we'll never bother you again," he explained.

Nancy couldn't believe her ears.

She had always wished that the boys would stop being such pests. Was her wish about to come true?

"No spitballs?" Nancy asked slowly.

The boys shook their heads.

"No straws up your nose during lunch?" Nancy asked. "Or gross noises?"

The boys shook their heads again.

Nancy took a deep breath. "No . . . Squirmy Wormies?" she asked.

David looked disappointed. "Aw, maybe just one or two—"

Jason nudged David. "No Squirmy Wormies. You have our word."

Nancy was delighted. But there was still one thing she had to know.

"Will you stop teasing Bess and George, too?" Nancy asked.

"Oh, come on!" Mike shouted.

Nancy folded her arms across her chest. "Well?" she asked. "Will you?"

"Yeah, yeah," David sighed.

Nancy gave a little jump.

Wait until I tell Bess and George, she thought. They'll be so psyched!

"Okay," Nancy said. "I'll investigate the footprint."

Mike held his hand up like a school crossing guard. "Not so fast," he said. "You first have to promise not to tell *anyone*. Especially Bess and George."

Nancy stared at the boys. "How can I work on a case without my best friends?" she asked. "We're a team."

Jason waved his hand. "Team shmeam," he said. "Is it a deal, or not?"

Nancy gave it a thought. If the boys kept their promise it would be great for her *and* her friends. Besides, Nancy loved solving mysteries more than anything.

"It's a deal," she said. "But since my friends can't help me, you will."

"How?" Jason asked.

"Lots of ways," Nancy said. "I once saw a dinosaur special on TV. People looking for fossils were pouring dirt in bags so they could sift through it."

"Boring!" Jason groaned.

"Then how about a trip after school to the River Heights Museum?" Nancy asked. "They have a real dinosaur skeleton from China. And lots of fossils, too."

"Forget it," Jason scoffed. "I have a better idea."

"What?" Nancy asked.

Jason's eyes lit up. *"Primeval Pests from the Prehistoric* is playing at the River Heights Cinema at four o'clock."

"It's about dinosaurs," Mike said.

"A movie?" Nancy asked. "You want to see a movie instead of going to a museum?"

Jason nodded. "Who needs a bunch of bones when you can see the real thing?"

Nancy gulped when she thought of going to the movies with Jason, David, and Mike. But a deal was a deal.

"Okay," she sighed. "I'll meet you at the movie house at three forty-five."

Jason turned to his friends. "After Nancy proves it's a real dinosaur footprint, they'll make a movie about *us!*"

The boys gave one another high-fives. Then they ran back to the playground.

Nancy stayed near the footprint. She pulled her blue notebook out of her jacket pocket. Turning to a fresh page she wrote the words "Prehistoric or Phony?"

Underneath Nancy drew two columns. One she labeled "Dinosaur." The other she labeled "Not a Dinosaur." In the end, the column with the most clues would prove if the footprint was real—or fake.

Nancy turned the page and sketched the footprint as best as she could.

The hardest part will be keeping it a secret from Bess and George, Nancy thought as she shut her notebook.

She ran back to the schoolyard and found Bess and George waiting for her.

"What happened?" Bess asked.

"Tell us everything," George said.

"Everything?" Nancy squeaked. She wanted to tell Bess and George about the footprint, but she couldn't.

"Um," Nancy said. "The boys found something under some bushes."

"I'll bet it was something gross," George said. "Like a squished bug."

"It *was* flat," Nancy said. She quickly

tried to change the subject. "Let's go on the swings."

"Okay," George said. The three girls hurried toward the swing set.

"I have an idea," Bess said as they ran. "Why don't we do something fun after school today."

Nancy was about to agree when she remembered the movie. "I can't," she said. "I have to . . . do something."

"What?" Bess asked.

Nancy stopped running. If she told her friends about the movie, she'd have to tell them all about the dinosaur case.

"I have to study for a quiz," Nancy said quickly. "Spelling."

"But Mrs. Reynolds isn't giving us a spelling quiz tomorrow," George said.

"She will someday." Nancy shrugged. "I want to be prepared."

George gave Nancy a funny look. The look said that she didn't really believe her.

This is the pits! Nancy thought. But when the boys stop bugging us, it will be worth it.

*   *   *

"Hannah?" Nancy asked in the car after school. "Were dinosaurs ever here in River Heights?"

Hannah Gruen, the Drews' housekeeper laughed as she steered the wheel. "I know I've been your housekeeper since you were three, Nancy," she said. "But I'm not *that* old!"

Nancy giggled. "I know, Hannah," she said. "It's just a question."

"Fair enough," Hannah said. She stopped at a red light. "I suppose there may have been dinosaurs here. But I'm sure glad I wasn't around to see them!"

The light changed, and Hannah drove into the cinema parking lot. After buying Nancy's ticket, she kissed her on the cheek. "I'll pick you up after the movie," she said. "In the meantime, have fun."

Nancy forced a smile. No way was she going to have fun with the boys!

"Prehistoric Pests," the ticket taker told Nancy. "That's in Theater Four."

"Thank you," Nancy said. She took her ticket stub and walked to the snack

16

stand, where she bought a small bag of popcorn.

"Nan-cy!" Jason's voice called out.

Nancy turned around. The boys were standing in front of the video games. They were holding jumbo popcorns, Panda bars, and boxes of Gooey Chewies.

Nancy walked over to them and frowned. "You're going to eat all *that*?"

"Nah," Mike said. He smiled slyly. "Just whatever we don't throw."

David tossed a popcorn at Mike. Mike tossed one back. Then the three boys began chasing one another through the lobby.

"Stop!" Nancy shouted. She began chasing them. "We're not here to play—we're here to study dinosaurs!"

The boys scooted around a corner. But when Nancy turned the corner—

CRASH! Her popcorn flew out of the bag as she bumped into someone hard. Stepping back, Nancy gulped when she saw who it was.

It was Bess—standing right next to George!

3

Zipped Lips

Yuck!" Bess cried. "You got buttered popcorn all over my new sweater, Nancy."

Nancy couldn't believe her bad luck. Of all people, she had to run into Bess and George.

"Sorry, Bess," Nancy said.

"What are you doing here?" George asked. "You said you wanted to study."

"I will," Nancy said. "But not now."

Bess smiled. She pointed to Theater Two. "Great!" she said. "Then we can all see *Diggety the Dog* together."

"I can't," Nancy said slowly. "I'm here to see . . . *Prehistoric Pests.*"

George looked surprised. "With who?"

"Naaaan-cy!" Jason's voice called.

Nancy gulped when she saw the boys waving at her from Theater Four.

"*Prehistoric Pests* is starting," David called. "We'll save you a seat!"

Nancy turned slowly to Bess and George. Their mouths were wide open.

"The boys?" Bess shrieked. "You're seeing *Prehistoric Pests* with the *boys?*"

"After all the creepy things they've done to us?" George asked.

Nancy felt awful. "I want to explain," she said. "But I can't yet."

"Let's go, Bess," George said. "*Diggety the Dog* is starting, too."

Nancy watched her friends walk away. Bess looked hurt as she glanced back.

What if this case spoils my friendship with Bess and George? Nancy thought sadly. And if it does—is it worth it?

Prehistoric Pests wasn't as bad as Nancy thought it would be. And the boys threw their popcorn only twice.

"Was that movie awesome or what?"

Jason asked as they came out of the movie theater. "Those dinosaurs were huge!"

"So were their feet!" Mike said. "And they had three toes—just like the footprint *we* found."

Nancy shook her head. "Those dinosaur feet were *much* bigger than the footprint you found."

The boys stared at Nancy.

"Are you saying that our footprint is *not* a dinosaur's?" Jason asked Nancy.

"I'm just saying that we have to explore all possibilities," Nancy said.

"Detective talk!" Jason scoffed.

"We just want to explore *one* possibility," Mike said. "That our footprint is for real."

"Yeah," Jason said. He folded his arms across his chest. "And you'd better prove that the footprint is a dinosaur's by Friday or the deal is off."

"O-f-f!" David spelled.

"But today is Tuesday," Nancy said. "That gives me only two more days!"

A car honked. It was Mrs. Hutchings picking the boys up in her minivan.

"Friday!" Jason repeated as they ran to the van.

Nancy felt her cheeks burn as she waited for Hannah to arrive.

Those boys think they're so smart, she thought. But I *am* going to prove this case by Friday.

Nancy pulled out her notebook. She wrote "too small" in the Not a Dinosaur column.

"I'm going to prove that the footprint is *not* a dinosaur's," Nancy muttered to herself. She closed her notebook and heaved a big sigh. "Now, if I can just figure out how."

"Daddy?" Nancy asked in the kitchen before dinner. "Do detectives have to know everything in order to be a detective?"

Carson Drew laughed as he sorted through the mail. "Nancy, if detectives knew everything, they wouldn't be detectives. They'd be superhuman!"

Nancy wished she could tell her dad about the case. Mr. Drew was a lawyer and always helped Nancy with her cases.

But this time Nancy couldn't tell anyone about the footprint—not even her dad.

"But what if a detective is working on a case," Nancy asked. "And needs to know more about the subject?"

"Then that detective should talk to an expert," Carson said. He smiled at Nancy. "Could that detective be you?"

"Maybe" was all Nancy could say. "Thanks, Daddy."

Nancy's puppy, Chocolate Chip, followed her into the den. Her father's advice was good, but it didn't help very much.

The only dinosaur experts I know are at the River Heights Museum, Nancy thought. And the boys don't want them to know about the footprint.

Nancy glanced at the clock. It was five-thirty—time for her favorite TV program, *Mr. Lizard's Funhouse*.

Oh, well, Nancy thought as she pressed the remote. Even detectives need a break sometimes.

Nancy smiled when Mr. Lizard appeared on the TV screen. He was wearing a checkered jacket and a baseball cap over his wild red hair.

"It's time for *Mr. Lizard's Funhouse!*" he said. "And as a special treat, we're going to start with the lizard dance!"

The music began, and Nancy jumped in front of the TV set. She wiggled her fingers over her head and flicked out her tongue. Chip barked and wagged her tail as she jumped up and down.

When the dance was over, Mr. Lizard walked over to a purple door. "Was that a knock I just heard?" he asked. "That must be my special guest!"

Mr. Lizard pulled the door open. A girl with dark hair stood in the doorway.

"She's nine-year-old Sylvie Arroyo, the winner of the junior statewide science fair!" Mr. Lizard announced.

I know Sylvie, Nancy thought. She's in the fourth grade at my school.

Sylvie was wearing a dinosaur cap, a dinosaur T-shirt, and dinosaur earrings.

"Let me guess," Mr. Lizard joked. "Your science project was about—pigs?"

"Dinosaurs!" Sylvie laughed. "I made a

dinosaur diorama out of all kinds of macaroni. I left it backstage."

"And it tasted *great!*" Mr. Lizard said. "Just kidding, just kidding."

Sylvie looked nervous as she followed Mr. Lizard into the TV clubhouse.

"So, Sylvie. What do you know about dinosaurs?" Mr. Lizard asked.

"I know that they first appeared over two hundred million years ago," Sylvie said. "And that dinosaur fossils have been found on every continent including Antarctica. And that they were once called the Great Lizards."

"Lizards?" Mr. Lizard cried. "I knew there was something about dinosaurs that I liked. Ha-ha-haaaa!"

Nancy stared at the TV set. Sylvie seemed to know everything about dinosaurs.

She was practically an expert. . . .

"That's it, Chip!" Nancy said excitedly. "I just found a dinosaur expert!"

4

Fossil Fever

The next morning Nancy couldn't wait to speak to Sylvie. She found her alone in the schoolyard at the water fountain.

"Hi, Sylvie," Nancy said.

Sylvie's chin dripped with water as she looked up. She was wearing a jacket with a shiny dinosaur stitched on the back.

"My name is Nancy Drew," Nancy said. "I'm in Mrs. Reynolds's class. I saw you on *Mr. Lizard's Funhouse* yesterday."

"He wears a wig. Did you know that?" Sylvie asked with wide eyes.

"Yes," Nancy said. "But can I talk to you about something else?"

"Can't," Sylvie said. She wiped her chin with her hand. "I have a meeting with my club. My *secret* club."

"Then can we talk later?" Nancy asked. "It's about dinosaurs."

Sylvie's eyes lit up at the word "dinosaurs." She pulled Nancy to the side and whispered: "I live at fifty-five Bank Street. Come to my house at three-thirty."

"Thanks!" Nancy called as Sylvie walked away. She was about to take a sip of water when she saw Bess and George.

Nancy felt relieved when she saw George smiling. Maybe her friends weren't mad at her anymore.

"Hi, Nancy," George said. "I remembered that I left my soccer ball in your yard last Saturday. Can I come over right after school to pick it up?"

"Maybe we can watch Mr. Lizard together," Bess said cheerfully.

"Great!" Nancy said. Then she remembered her meeting with Sylvie. "I mean, I can't. I'm busy after school."

"Again?" Bess complained.

"Hey, Nancy!" a voice called out.

Nancy whirled around. She saw Jason, David, and Mike running over.

"I'll bet I know who you're busy *with*," George said angrily.

"The boys," Bess sneered.

"I can explain," Nancy said. She shook her head. "No, I can't! I mean, I'll bring your soccer ball to school tomorrow, George. I promise!"

George didn't say a word. She and Bess huffed away just as the boys ran over.

"Hey, Nancy," Jason said. "Did you solve the case yet?"

"It's Wednesday," Mike pointed out. "One day closer to Friday."

"I haven't solved the case yet," Nancy said. "But I found someone who might be able to help us."

"Nuh-uh," Jason said. "You promised you wouldn't tell anyone."

"I won't," Nancy said. "But we can still ask Sylvie about dinosaurs."

"Who's Sylvie?" David asked.

"She's a dinosaur expert," Nancy explained. "She invited me to her house after school. You should come, too."

"To a *girl's* house?" Jason sneered.

"No way!" Mike said. He wrinkled his nose. "She might make us play with dolls."

Nancy planted her hands on her hips. "Sylvie Arroyo is a state science fair winner!" she declared.

"Science?" Mike said. "That reminds me—they're giving away free Squirmy Wormies at the Science Nook after school."

The boys gave each other high-fives. "Squirmy Wormies! Squirmy Wormies! Squirmy Wormies!" they sang as they ran away.

"You're not helping me!" Nancy shouted. She threw back her head and groaned. Why did she agree to take this case? Why? Why? Why?

Bess and George ignored Nancy the whole day. Nancy ate lunch and spent recess with Katie Zaleski and Rebecca Ramirez. Nancy liked Katie and Rebecca, but she still missed Bess and George.

When school was over Nancy went

straight home. After a quick snack and permission from Hannah, Nancy walked the three blocks to Sylvie's house.

"Sylvie is in the backyard with her friends," Mrs. Arroyo told Nancy. "You can go back there if you'd like."

"Thanks, Mrs. Arroyo," Nancy said. She walked around the house. She expected to find Sylvie and her friends playing ball or a board game, but she was wrong.

"Dig faster!" Sylvie shouted.

Nancy gasped. Six kids were digging through Sylvie's backyard with plastic shovels and spoons.

"I'm going to find a dinosaur if it's the last thing I do!" Sylvie wailed to herself. "A Stegasaurus! A Kentrosaurus! I'll even settle for a puny Mussaurus!"

"Hi, Sylvie," Nancy called.

Sylvie whirled around. "You want to join the Dino Squad, don't you?" she asked.

"What's the Dino Squad?" Nancy asked.

"I thought you knew," Sylvie said, surprised. She turned to a boy digging nearby. "Tell her, Jared."

31

Jared took a deep breath. "Members of the Dino Squad share one important goal—to find the ultimate fossil."

"Sylvie, I found something!" a red-haired boy with a plastic shovel called. "I think it's an egg!"

"An egg!" Sylvie shrieked.

The boy ran over. He was holding a white oval-shaped object covered with dirt. "It's probably from a duck-billed Edmontosaurus," he said.

"That's the best kind, Marty!" Sylvie exclaimed. She carefully took the object in her hands.

"I have to tap it," Sylvie said. "There might be a fossil inside."

Excited whispers filled the yard.

"Will somebody please hold the egg while I tap it?" Sylvie asked.

Hmm, Nancy thought. Maybe if I do something nice for Sylvie, she'll tell me all about dinosaurs.

"I will," Nancy offered.

"Okay, but be very careful," Sylvie said. "Fossils are very delicate."

Nancy carefully took the earth-covered

32

object. It didn't feel like a real egg—more like plastic.

Sylvie raised a spoon. She was about to tap when Nancy noticed something gross. A tiny worm had crawled from the dirt-covered egg and onto Nancy's hand.

"Gross!" Nancy cried. She wiggled her fingers and—CRASH—the egg fell to the ground!

"You ruined it!" Sylvie shrieked. "Now my dinosaur egg is cracked in half!"

"Um, Sylvie?" a girl with black hair said. "I don't think it's a dinosaur egg."

Nancy peered down at the egg. Instead of a fossil spilling out, there was brightly wrapped candy.

"Did you once have an Easter egg hunt in your backyard?" Marty asked.

Sylvie blushed a deep shade of red.

"Okay, so it's not a dinosaur egg," she said. "But at least we won't have to sit on it and hatch it. Right?"

The kids mumbled in agreement as they returned to their digging.

"Sylvie?" Nancy asked. "Do you think dinosaurs roamed here in River Heights?"

Sylvie's eyes flashed. "Dinosaurs roamed everywhere!" she exclaimed.

"And they were all gigantic, right?" Nancy asked. "Like hundreds of feet high?"

"Not all," Sylvie said. "Some were as small as dogs. Even as small as chickens."

"No way!" Nancy gasped.

"Why do you want to know?" Sylvie asked Nancy. She seemed worried. "Did you find something? A bone? A dinosaur tooth?"

The other kids began surrounding Nancy. It made her a bit nervous.

"Because if you found a fossil," Marty said, "we want to know about it."

Nancy gulped. The last thing she could tell them was about the footprint.

"I have got to go now," Nancy said quickly. She gave a little wave. "Bye!"

All eyes were on Nancy as she left the yard. When she was a block away she took out her detective notebook.

"If dinosaurs came in all sizes," Nancy said to herself. "Then maybe the boys are right. Maybe the footprint *is* a dinosaur's!"

5

Tooth or Dare

Nancy sat in the den after dinner. She flipped through a colorful book about dinosaurs. The book had belonged to her dad when he was in the third grade.

"Wow!" Nancy said to herself. "Look at the size of that!"

She placed her finger on a picture of a dinosaur jaw. The fossil had big curved and pointy teeth.

I'll bet Sylvie would love to find that, Nancy thought.

Just then Nancy heard Chip barking in the yard. She ran outside and found her puppy holding something between her teeth.

"Not now, girl," Nancy said with a smile. "It's too late to play catch."

Chip dropped the object at Nancy's feet. She picked it up. The object was big and curved. At one end it was pointy. At the other end it was flat.

Just like—

"A dinosaur tooth?" Nancy gasped. She carried the object into the house and compared it to the picture. They were almost exactly alike!

Wait, Nancy told herself. A good detective never jumps to conclusions. That's what Daddy always says.

Nancy opened her detective notebook. In the Dinosaur column she drew a tiny picture of the object. Then she wrote the word "Tooth" with a question mark.

Was it a dinosaur tooth or not? Nancy didn't know. That's why she had to show it to someone—and fast.

The River Heights Museum, Nancy thought. I'll bring the tooth there.

Nancy shut her notebook and smiled.

The boys said she couldn't show the footprint to the museum. But they never said anything about a tooth.

That night Nancy was so excited about the tooth that she could hardly sleep. When she went to school the next morning she tried hard to keep her new secret.

I'm not telling anyone yet, Nancy thought on her way to her classroom. Not even the boys.

"Hey, Nancy!" Mike called in the hallway. "Check it out!"

Nancy whirled around. Jason was holding a bulky plastic garbage bag.

"What's that?" Nancy asked.

"Dirt," Jason said. "You told us that dinosaur hunters sift through dirt for fossils. So we dug this up from around the footprint."

"In case there are any dinosaur bones or something," David added.

Nancy smiled. The boys were finally doing some work for a change.

"Good," Nancy said. "We can sift through it during recess."

"Recess—no way!" David cried. "We're supposed to play dodge ball today."

"But tell us what you find," Jason said. He shoved the bag into Nancy's arms.

"Wait!" Nancy shouted as the boys ran down the hallway. "You can't leave me with this!"

Nancy groaned as she lugged the bag over to her cubby. She was about to shove it inside when she felt George tap her shoulder. Bess was with her.

"Did you bring in my soccer ball?" George asked Nancy.

Nancy bit her lip. She had been so busy thinking about the tooth that she had forgotten all about George's soccer ball.

"George, I—" Nancy started to say.

Bess pointed to the bag in Nancy's hands. "That's probably it," she said.

George reached for the plastic bag in Nancy's hands. "Thanks. I'll take it."

The dirt, Nancy thought. Oh, no!

"You can't have it, George," Nancy said.

Bess jumped back as George began to tug at the bag. "Why not? It's mine and I need it for soccer practice!"

"George, it's not your soccer ball!" Nancy insisted. Other kids were gathering around to watch the tug-of-war.

"It *is* my soccer ball. Give it to me!" George demanded. She gave the bag one hard pull.

RRRRRRRIP!! The bag tore. Dirt poured all over the floor and George's sneakers.

"Yuck!" George cried. She wiggled her feet to shake off the dirt. "Was this your idea, Nancy?"

"No," Nancy said. "It was the boys' idea. I mean—"

"The boys—I knew it!" George interrupted. "Come on, Bess. Before she throws Squirmy Wormies in our hair."

"I wouldn't!" Nancy gasped as her friends walked away. "Never!"

"Uh-oh," said Kyle Leddington from her class. "Here comes Mrs. Reynolds."

"And *trouble*," Peter DeSands said.

"What a mess," Mrs. Reynolds said. She looked at the dirt and shook her head.

"It was an accident, Mrs. Reynolds," Nancy explained.

"Was this for a flower you were going to plant, Nancy?" Mrs. Reynolds asked.

Nancy opened her mouth to speak, but nothing came out.

"All right, then," Mrs. Reynolds said. "Go to Mr. Ingstrom's office and tell him about this, please."

"Yes, Mrs. Reynolds," Nancy said.

She was glad her teacher was sending her to the custodian's office and not to the principal's.

Nancy hurried down the hallway. When she reached Mr. Ingstrom's office she found the door shut. She was about to knock when she heard the custodian talking to someone.

"So, Enid," Mr. Ingstrom was saying. "What's this about a big surprise?"

Nancy knew that *Enid* was Mrs. Carmichael's first name.

"Oh, it *will* be a surprise, Bob," Mrs. Carmichael answered. "When everyone sees that dinosaur they're going to flip!"

Nancy gasped.

Dinosaur? Did she just say "dinosaur"?

6

Dino-Saw!

What dinosaur? Nancy thought. And how can that be? Dinosaurs are extinct!

Nancy jumped as the door flew open.

"Nancy!" Mrs. Carmichael said. She walked out of the office and smiled. "What a nice surprise."

"Hi, Mrs. Carmichael," Nancy said in a squeaky voice. She wanted to ask her about the dinosaur, but it wasn't polite to snoop. "B-b-bye, Mrs. Carmichael."

After apologizing to Mr. Ingstrom about the dirt, Nancy hurried back to her classroom. On the way she stopped to open her detective notebook.

In the Dinosaur column she wrote "Mrs. Carmichael's Surprise."

Maybe Mrs. Carmichael didn't say dinosaur, Nancy thought as she stared at the page. Maybe she said . . . cole slaw.

Nancy studied the two columns and sighed. Now there were no clues in the Not a Dinosaur column. Zero! Zip!

Who cares? Nancy thought. All I want to do is solve this case. And most of all — get my best friends back.

Nancy stopped at her cubby to take out a pencil. But when she reached inside she found a note. It was on blue stationery with white designs and was folded into a neat square.

Nancy opened the note. Inside it read, "Don't go where you don't belong!"

Nancy stared at the angry words. The note was written on a computer, but she had a pretty good idea who had left it.

Bess and George, Nancy thought. They're telling me not to hang around the boys anymore.

Nancy felt a lump in her throat. She slipped the note in her pocket.

And they're probably right!

During recess Nancy got permission to go to the school library. There she looked at more pictures of dinosaur teeth. She was almost sure that the object Chip had dug up was a real dinosaur tooth.

"Next stop, River Heights Museum," Nancy whispered to herself.

When school was over Nancy ran straight home for the tooth. Then Hannah drove her to the River Heights Museum.

"If it's a real dinosaur tooth, you'll be rich, Nancy," Hannah told Nancy in the car.

"How come?" Nancy asked.

Hannah nodded to the dinosaur tooth in Nancy's lap. "Can you imagine how much the tooth fairy will leave for *that*?"

Nancy giggled as Hannah parked the car. They stepped out and walked through the glass doors of the museum.

"I'm going to find someone who I can show this tooth to, Hannah," Nancy said.

"Okay," Hannah said. "Meet me at the butterfly exhibit in twenty minutes."

Nancy checked her watch. After saying goodbye to Hannah she saw a man with dark hair and a mustache. He wore a museum badge on his blue jacket.

"Sir?" Nancy asked. "I think I found a dinosaur fossil. Who can I show it to?"

"That would be me," the man answered. "I'm Dr. Jacobs, the museum's paleontologist."

"Pay-lee-what?" Nancy asked.

"Pa-le-on-tol-o-gist," Dr. Jacobs repeated. "A person who studies dinosaurs."

"That's a big word!" Nancy said.

"So were dinosaurs." Dr. Jacobs shrugged. "Now, what can I do for you?"

Nancy held up the dinosaur tooth. "My dog found this in our yard. I thought it looked like a dinosaur tooth."

Dr. Jacobs put on a pair of glasses. He took the tooth from Nancy and turned it over in his hand. "Oh, yes," he said. "It definitely is a dinosaur tooth."

"Yes!" Nancy cheered.

Dr. Jacobs handed Nancy the tooth.

"And there are plenty more where that came from," he added.

Nancy's mouth dropped open. "More?" she asked. "In . . . my yard?"

"In our gift shop," Dr. Jacobs corrected. "Follow me."

Gift shop? Now Nancy was totally confused. She followed Dr. Jacobs through the lobby and into the museum gift shop.

"You see?" Dr. Jacobs said. He waved his hand over a row of shelves. "These casts are our best sellers. Aside from the dinosaur egg pencil sharpeners."

Nancy stared at the objects on the shelves. Each one looked exactly like the tooth she'd found in her yard.

"The casts were made by pouring plaster of paris over real dinosaur teeth," Dr. Jacobs went on. "The real teeth are in a museum in New York City."

"Oh," Nancy said quietly. It was hard to hide her disappointment.

"Any other questions?" Dr. Jacobs asked.

Nancy really wanted to ask Dr. Jacobs about the footprint in the schoolyard, but she knew she couldn't.

"No, Dr. Jacobs," Nancy said. "But thanks for your help."

As Dr. Jacobs left, Nancy was still confused. Even if the tooth was just a cast—how did it get into her backyard?

Nancy glanced around the colorful gift shop. It was filled with lots of dinosaur things—pencils with dinosaur erasers, rubber dinosaur slippers, even dinosaur earrings.

A salesgirl smiled at Nancy from behind the counter. "If you like dinosaurs," she said, "then check out this dinosaur stationery."

The salesgirl handed Nancy a clear box filled with blue paper. Then she left to help another customer.

Nancy studied the blue stationery with the white shapes. She thought the shapes were clouds until she looked closer. They were all kinds of dinosaurs.

This paper looks familiar, Nancy thought. Where have I seen it before?

Suddenly Nancy remembered the note in her cubby. She pulled it out of her pocket and compared it to the stationery.

It was exactly the same!

That's funny, Nancy thought.

Bess's stationery is pink with yellow butterflies. And George's stationery has a soccer ball design. Neither one owns dinosaur stationery.

Nancy stared at the note.

Unless Bess and George *didn't* write the note, she thought.

But then, who did?

"So, is it a real dinosaur tooth, Nancy?" Hannah asked as they drove home.

"No." Nancy looked down at the tooth in her lap. "Just a cast of one."

"Oh, well," Hannah joked. "At least you won't have to brush it twice a day."

"Cute, Hannah." Nancy smiled.

When they reached the house Nancy stayed outside. She wanted to find George's soccer ball once and for all.

"Now, where did George last kick it?" Nancy asked Chip as she searched the yard.

All of a sudden something strange caught Nancy's eye.

In the ground was a footprint. A giant footprint with three pointy toes!

Nancy stared at the footprint. Then she glanced around. There were many weird footprints—all over the ground!

"Dinosaurs!" Nancy gasped. "In my own front yard!"

7

Three Toes—Who Goes?

Nancy tried to stay calm. She compared the footprints on the ground to the drawing in her notebook.

"Wide feet, pointy toes," Nancy said to herself. "A definite match!"

All of the footprints seemed to lead around the house to the Drews' backyard.

Nancy took a deep breath as she slipped her notebook into her pocket.

"Come on, Chip," Nancy said in a hushed voice. "Let's follow those footprints."

Very quietly Nancy and Chip walked around to the backyard. The trails fanned out in different directions.

Nancy's eyes followed one trail. Then she froze. Sticking out from behind a tree was a giant green foot—with pointy purple toenails!

She stepped back. She was about to call for her dad when Chip dashed toward the tree.

"Chip!" Nancy shouted. "Come back!"

Chip stood at the tree and growled.

"Go awaaaaay!" yelled a voice from behind the tree. "Beat it! Scram!"

A talking dinosaur? Nancy thought.

Her mouth dropped open as Sylvie Arroyo stumbled out. On her feet were the dinosaur slippers from the gift shop.

"Woof! Woof!" Chip barked. She began nibbling on Sylvie's slippers.

"Help meeee!" Sylvie yelled.

Nancy watched as six more heads popped out from behind bushes and trees.

"The Dino Squad!" Nancy gasped.

The kids ran to help Sylvie. They were *all* wearing green dinosaur slippers.

"What are you doing here?" Nancy demanded as she tugged Chip away.

Marty pointed to his foot. "What does it

look like we're doing?" he asked. "We're making tracks."

"Tracks?" Nancy asked. "Why?"

A younger girl shrugged. "Because Sylvie told us to," she said.

The yard was so quiet you could hear a leaf drop. Everyone stared at Sylvie.

"Okay, it was my idea," Sylvie told Nancy. "I thought that if we planted enough fake fossils and footprints, you'd be too busy to look for a *real* dinosaur."

"And *we* want to be the first kids to find a real dinosaur fossil," the boy named Jared explained.

Just like Jason, David, and Mike, Nancy thought with a sigh.

"What difference does it make who finds a dinosaur fossil as long as it's found?" Nancy asked. "Then everyone can study it. And learn from it, too."

Everyone was silent.

A girl wearing glasses turned to Sylvie. "She's right, you know."

"Yeah," a boy with a baseball cap said. "We've been trying so hard to find a fossil that dinosaurs aren't fun anymore."

"I want to make more macaroni dinosaurs!" the younger girl cried.

"Okay, okay," Sylvie said, waving her arms. "You win. Less work. More fun."

Nancy planted her hands on her hips. "Does this mean you won't leave any more fake fossils in my yard?" she asked.

"Nah," Marty said. "We ran out of stuff from the museum gift shop anyway."

The gift shop! Nancy thought of the note and the dinosaur stationery.

"Sylvie?" Nancy asked. "Did you also leave a note in my cubby, telling me I shouldn't go where I don't belong?"

The curly-haired girl raised her hand. "I did," she said. "Sorry."

Nancy should have been mad but instead she was glad. The angry note *wasn't* from Bess and George!

"Hey, Dino Squad," Sylvie announced. "There's a new flavor at the Double Dip. It's called Flaky Fossil Crunch."

"Now, *that* sounds like fun," Marty declared. "Let's go for it!"

The dinosaur feet made thumping sounds as the kids ran from the yard.

"Well, that explains who left the phony tooth and the note," Nancy said to Chip. "But it still doesn't explain the weird footprint behind the school."

Nancy's job was far from over. And the next day was Friday. If she didn't prove anything by then, the boys' deal would be off!

She wished she could tell Bess and George about the footprint, but a promise was a promise—even with the boys!

Nancy walked around to the front yard. She found George's soccer ball under a bush.

Nancy was about to pick up the ball when she got an idea.

"Hmmm," Nancy said. "Maybe I don't have to show Bess and George the footprint behind the school. Maybe they can find it themselves!"

"Bess! George!" Nancy called the next morning. She ran through the schoolyard with George's soccer ball under her arm.

"My soccer ball," George said. "You finally brought it in."

"Want to practice kicking in back of the school?" Nancy asked.

"Why don't you ask the boys?" Bess said with a smirk.

"Because *you're* my best friends, not them," Nancy said. "Come on."

Bess and George followed Nancy behind the school.

"I'll kick the ball over to you," Nancy told George. She placed the ball on the ground. But instead of kicking it to George she kicked it toward the bushes. It flew past George and rolled right under the bush covering the strange footprint.

Perfect! Nancy thought.

"Hel-lo?" George called, waving her hands. "I'm over here!"

Nancy pretended to be embarrassed. "Whoops!" she said.

"I'll get the ball," Bess called. She ran over to the bush and brushed it aside.

Nancy held her breath. She began to count to herself. One. Two. Three—

"Look what I found!" Bess cried.

58

All systems go! Nancy cheered to herself. She and George ran over to Bess. They kneeled down beside her.

"Check out that crazy footprint in the rock." George whistled. "You don't see that everyday!"

"What kind of a footprint is that?" Bess asked. She looked nervous.

"I don't know." Nancy shrugged. "Maybe a bear's. Or . . . a dinosaur's?"

"Dinosaur?" Bess cried. She jumped up and accidentally kicked the soccer ball. It rolled deeper under the bush.

"It's okay. I'll get it," Nancy said. She brushed aside the bush and saw something she hadn't seen before. It was a name scratched into the rock.

The name was *Enid*.

"That's weird," Nancy said slowly. "That wasn't here before."

"How do you know?" George asked. "And who's Enid?"

"The only Enid I know is Mrs. Carmichael," Nancy said. Then her eyes lit up. Mrs. Carmichael had spoken about a dinosaur yesterday. Maybe she knew something about the footprint.

"Bess, George," Nancy said. "We have to go to the lunchroom right now. We have to speak to Mrs. Carmichael."

"But it's Friday," George said. "The reunion breakfast is going on. And Mrs. Carmichael is in charge."

"I know," Nancy said. "But this is important."

Bess tilted her head. "Do you know something we don't know, Nancy?"

"Yes," Nancy said. "And I'll explain everything. Soon!"

The girls got permission to visit Mrs. Carmichael. They hurried through the hallway past the murals and trophy cases.

The smell of breakfast filled the air as they neared the lunchroom.

"Pancakes and maple syrup!" Bess cried. "If we ask, maybe Mrs. Carmichael will give us some."

Bess started to run toward the lunchroom. She froze near the door.

"Bess?" Nancy asked. "What's wrong?"

Bess's hand shook as she pointed. "N-N-Nancy!" she stammered. "Look!"

Nancy looked to see where Bess was pointing. Then she froze, too.

Sticking out of the lunchroom door was a long green tail with yellow spikes.

A dinosaur tail!

8

Mrs. Carmichael's Surprise

A dinosaur!" Nancy gasped.

The girls clutched one another and stepped back.

"W-w-what's a dinosaur doing in our lunchroom?" Bess asked.

"Maybe he likes pancakes," George said.

The tail wiggled. The girls screamed and ran down the hall.

"Hey, now!" a voice called out. "No running in the hall!"

Nancy stopped. She turned around slowly and gasped. Standing in front of the lunchroom was Mrs. Carmichael wearing a big green dinosaur suit.

"Mrs. Carmichael?" George asked. "Is that you?"

"What's the matter?" Mrs. Carmichael joked. "Don't you recognize me without my hairnet? Ha-ha-haaaa!"

Nancy blinked hard. Mrs. Carmichael's head was covered with a green hood. There was a hole cut out in the front for her face. Her body was big, green, and bulky. In her clawlike hands was a red yearbook.

As Mrs. Carmichael walked over, Nancy noticed something else—her big dinosaur feet had three pointy toes.

Just like the footprint behind the school! Nancy thought excitedly.

"Is that your new uniform, Mrs. Carmichael?" Bess asked with a gulp.

"This used to be my *mascot* costume when I was a sixth grader here at Carl Sandburg," Mrs. Carmichael explained. "I wore it just for the reunion today."

"This school had a mascot?" George asked excitedly. "What sport?"

"Basketball," Mrs. Carmichael said. "The sixth-grade Crocodiles used to play the fifth-grade Kangaroos. I thought the Crocs could use some spirit, so I looked all over town for a crocodile suit."

"Did you find one?" Bess asked.

Mrs. Carmichael shook her head. "The closest thing to a crocodile was this dinosaur suit," she said. "So I became Doogie the Dinosaur—school mascot."

"How come it still fits you?" Bess asked. "I mean . . . it's a pretty big suit."

"I was a big sixth grader," Mrs. Carmichael said. She opened the yearbook. "Big enough to play basketball. But they didn't have a girl's team in those days."

Nancy looked at a black-and-white picture in the yearbook. There was a young Mrs. Carmichael dressed up as Doogie.

Nancy pointed to the feet in the picture. "We found a footprint just like that in back of the school," she said.

Mrs. Carmichael laughed. "That was mine," she said. "There used to be an old playground in back of the school. One day when they were repaving it I accidentally ran across the wet cement in my costume."

Nancy's heart beat with excitement. That explained the weird footprint. But she still had another question.

"Did you also write your name in the cement, Mrs. Carmichael?" Nancy asked.

Mrs. Carmichael nodded. "Some Crocodiles dared me and I did it." She sighed. "Big mistake."

"Why? Did you get in trouble?" Bess asked with wide eyes.

"Sure did," Mrs. Carmichael said. "I couldn't be Doogie anymore."

A man with a mustache stuck his head out of the lunchroom door. "Hey, Enid!" he said. "We're running out of fish sticks!"

Mrs. Carmichael winked at the girls. "Time to get back to my party," she said.

"Wait, Mrs. Carmichael," Nancy said.

"May I please borrow your yearbook? I'll return it later at lunch."

"Sure," Mrs. Carmichael said. She handed Nancy the yearbook. Then she dragged her long tail into the lunch-room.

"Yes!" Nancy cheered. She clutched the yearbook to her chest. "Case closed!"

"Case?" George asked. "Were you working on a case all this time, Nancy?"

"Without us?" Bess asked.

The bell rang and the main door swung open. Nancy saw Jason, David, and Mike running inside with the other kids.

"I'll explain everything in just a minute," Nancy promised.

George waved her arms in the air. "You keep saying that!" she complained.

Nancy knew that was true. She ran to the boys and held up the yearbook.

"Ta-daaa!" Nancy sang. She pointed to the picture of Doogie. "Check it out."

The boys eyed the picture.

"A kid in a dinosaur suit," Jason said. "So what?"

Nancy took a deep breath and explained everything.

"You mean it wasn't a *real* dinosaur footprint?" David asked.

"It was Mrs. Carmichael?" Mike cried.

The boys were silent for a few seconds. Then Jason heaved a big sigh.

"Okay, so you solved the case," he said. "Big deal."

"It *is* a big deal," Nancy said. "Now you can't bug me or my friends again!"

The boys shook their heads.

"That was only if you proved it *was* a real dinosaur," Jason sneered.

"And you didn't," Mike said.

Nancy couldn't believe her ears. "What?" she cried.

"The deal is off," David said. He grinned and tossed a handful of Squirmy Wormies onto Nancy's head. "O-f-f!"

"Squirmy Wormies! Squirmy Wormies! Squirmy Wormies!" the boys sang as they ran away.

Nancy bit her lip as a green rubber worm slid down her nose. All that hard work for nothing.

But she wasn't very angry.

No one *made* me work on this case, Nancy thought as she brushed away the worms. It was my own choice.

She walked back to her friends and smiled. "News flash," she announced. "I will never hang out with Jason, David, and Mike again!"

"Cool!" George said.

"Then let's all go to the Double Dip after school," Bess said excitedly. "Just like best friends again.

The words "best friends" made Nancy's heart fly. "Okay," she said. "But there's one flavor I do *not* want to try."

"Which one?" Bess asked.

"Flaky Fossil Crunch!" Nancy laughed. The three best friends hooked arms and skipped to their classroom together.

Nancy was still smiling as she slid into her seat. She pulled out her detective notebook and opened it across her desk. Then she began to write:

Daddy was right. A good detective should never jump to conclusions, whether it's about a weird footprint or a creepy note.

One more thing I learned on this case. Dinosaurs may be extinct, but good friendships last forever and ever and ever!

Case closed.

EASY TO READ—FUN TO SOLVE!

**Meet up with suspense and mystery
in The Hardy Boys® are:**

THE CLUES™ BROTHERS

Available from Minstrel® Books
Published by Pocket Books

2389

Sabrina
The Teenage Witch®

Salem's Tails®

What's it like to be a powerful warlock,
sentenced to one hundred years in a
cat's body for trying to take over the world?

Ask Salem.

**Read all about Salem's magical
adventures in this series based on the hit
ABC-TV show!**

A MINSTREL® BOOK
Published by Pocket Books